ISABEL'S CAR WA$H

Sheila Bair

Illustrated by Judy Stead

www.av2books.com

Your AV² Media Enhanced book gives you a fiction readalong online. Log on to www.av2books.com and enter the unique book code from this page to use your readalong.

AV² Readalong Navigation

Go to **www.av2books.com**, and enter this book's unique code.

BOOK CODE

Q779369

AV² by Weigl brings you media enhanced books that support active learning.

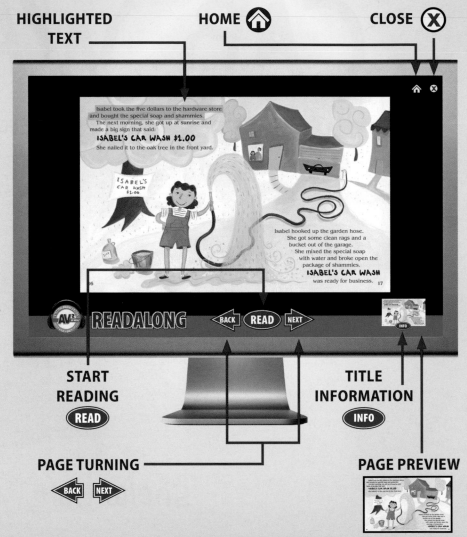

HIGHLIGHTED TEXT

HOME

CLOSE

START READING
READ

TITLE INFORMATION
INFO

PAGE TURNING
BACK NEXT

PAGE PREVIEW

First Published by

ALBERT WHITMAN & COMPANY
Publishing children's books since 1919

Published by AV² by Weigl
350 5ᵗʰ Avenue, 59ᵗʰ Floor New York, NY 10118
Copyright ©2013 AV² by Weigl

Printed in the United States of America in North Mankato, Minnesota
1 2 3 4 5 6 7 8 9 0 16 15 14 13 12

Text copyright © 2008 by Sheila Bair.
Illustrations copyright © 2008 by Judy Stead.
Published in 2008 by Albert Whitman & Company

052012
WEP160512

Library of Congress Cataloging-in-Publication Data

Bair, Sheila.
Isabel's car wa$h / by Sheila Bair ; illustrated by Judy Stead.
p. cm.
Summary: To earn money to buy a doll that she wants, Isabel starts a car wash business with money invested by her friends, hoping to make a profit for everyone. Includes information on selling shares in a business.
ISBN 978-1-61913-118-7 (hard cover : alk. paper)
[1. Car washes--Fiction. 2. Moneymaking projects--Fiction. 3. Business enterprises--Fiction.] I. Stead, Judy, ill. II. Title. III. Title: Isabel's car wash.
PZ7.B1617Is 2012
[E]--dc23
2012016948

For Scott.—s.b.

For Steadly, best CFO (Chief Family Officer), with love.—j.s.

Sheila Bair's current and former jobs include
Chairman, Federal Deposit Insurance Corporation; Professor of Finance,
University of Massachusetts; Assistant Secretary of the U.S. Treasury; and
Senior Vice President, New York Stock Exchange.
She is also the author of *Rock, Brock, and the Savings Shock*.

TOYS

NEW!
NELLY
LONGHAIR
$10.00

4

Isabel Dinero wanted a Nelly Longhair doll more than anything in the world. Nelly was on sale at Murphy's Toys for ten dollars. Isabel only had fifty cents. She needed to earn some money. But how?

5

She wasn't old enough to baby-sit. She didn't even know how to change a dirty diaper. Yuk!
She couldn't mow lawns. She wasn't strong enough to push the lawn mower.

She thought about walking
the neighbor's dog. But he was
too big. He would walk *her!*
What could she do?

Isabel thought and thought about how to earn some money. Walking home from school the next day, she thought about it so hard that SPLAT!— she marched into a big puddle. The water came from a nearby car wash. There were lots of cars lined up there. The weather had been terrible, and everyone's car was grimy.

"So many people wanting to wash
their cars," Isabel said to herself.

9

Suddenly she had a great idea. She could open a car wash at her house! She'd helped her brother Miguel wash his car in the driveway lots of times.

All she needed was the special car-washing soap her brother used, and those fancy towels he called "shammies" to dry the cars off.

Isabel headed right to the hardware store to buy the soap and shammies. She put her two quarters on the counter. But when the man rang up the bill, it was five dollars!

How could she get five dollars?

 Isabel remembered that once
five friends had each given her a
quarter when she lost her school
lunch money.

Her mom gave her five quarters to pay them back
and another five dimes for a little extra each. Isabel's
friends were really happy to get the extra money.

Maybe those same five friends would each give her
a dollar to join her in starting her car wash.
In return, she'd share some of the money she made.
Isabel just knew she could make enough money to
buy Nelly *and* pay her friends back, plus a little more.

Isabel's parents said OK to her plan. So the next day, she asked each of her friends for a dollar.

Her friends weren't sure they wanted to give up their money. They had things they wanted to buy like comics, ice cream, and Go Fish cards.

"If you give me your dollars," Isabel told them, "I think I can pay you back, plus more."

"Do you know how to wash cars?" asked Mary Kay.

"Yes, I've helped my brother lots of times," answered Isabel.

"What if no one comes to your car wash?" asked Tyler.

"But they will," said Isabel. "With all the rain we've had, everyone's car is muddy."

"How will you divide the money you make?" asked Raj.

Isabel thought for a moment. "I will keep half and split the other half with you."

"Why should you get more?" asked Natalie.

"Because it's my idea, and I will do all the work," answered Isabel.

"But if not enough people come to your car wash, we could lose our money," said Lin.

"That *is* a risk," said Isabel. "But a car wash is a good idea, and I'll work very hard."

Her friends looked at each other.

"We know you'll work hard," said Mary Kay.

"So we'll take the risk," said Tyler.

"But we sure hope you know what you're doing," said Natalie.

Everyone gave Isabel one dollar. Now she had five dollars.

Isabel took the five dollars to the hardware store and bought the special soap and shammies.

The next morning, she got up at sunrise and made a big sign that said:

ISABEL'S CAR WASH $1.00

She nailed it to the oak tree in the front yard.

Isabel hooked up the garden hose.
She got some clean rags and a
bucket out of the garage.
She mixed the special soap
with water and broke open the
package of shammies.
ISABEL'S CAR WASH
was ready for business. 17

Isabel's stomach was in a knot as she waited for her first customer. Finally, at 9:30, Mrs. Pristine from across the street drove up. "One dollar for a car wash," she squealed. "Such a bargain!"

Isabel scrubbed Mrs. Pristine's car sparkling clean—and earned her first dollar. She did such a good job that Mrs. Pristine called up her friends and told them about the car wash. Then they told their friends, and the news spread.

19

Lots of people came to Isabel's car wash.
"Such a bargain," everyone said.
The cars kept coming and coming.
Isabel worked and worked. Her fingers got red and puckered like raisins. Her sneakers got soggy and rubbed blisters on her heels.

Isabel washed:

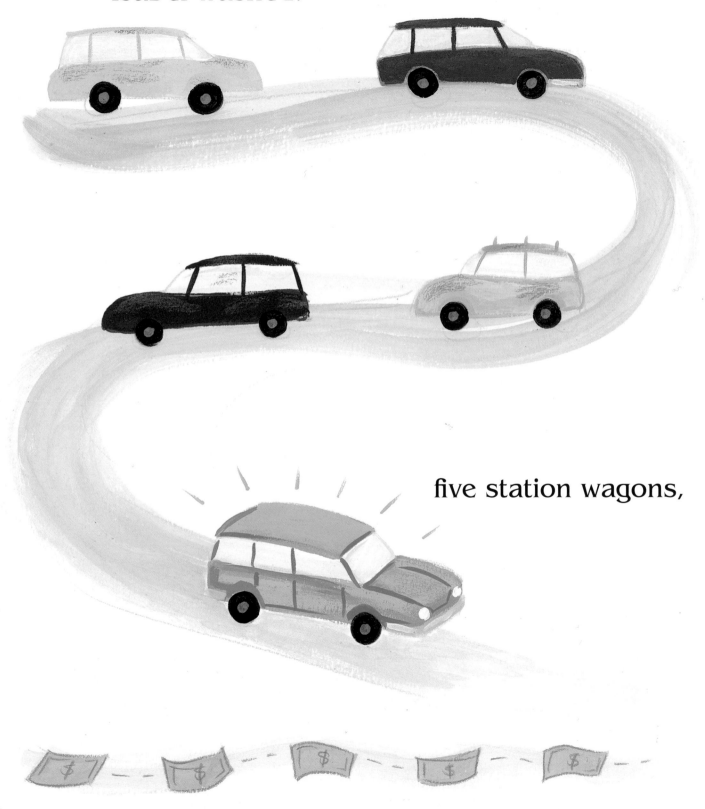

five station wagons,

two minivans,

three punch buggies,

three convertibles
(with the tops up),

one pickup truck,

one golf cart,

two pedal cars, one go-cart, and

. . . a dog? (Little Joey from next door brought over his dog.)

"Should have charged *two* dollars," Isabel muttered.

She finished just before dinnertime.
She counted up her money and found
that she had twenty crisp one-dollar bills.
She was pooped!

27

The next day, Isabel invited her five friends over. Just as she'd promised, she paid them half of the money she'd made and kept the other half for herself. Half of twenty dollars came to ten dollars—or two dollars for each friend.

"I doubled your money!" Isabel said proudly.

Her friends were all happy. Isabel was happy, too. She had ten dollars left over to buy Nelly Longhair. She put her ten dollars into her purse and set off for Murphy's Toys.

When she reached the checkout counter, the lady said, "Ten dollars and fifty cents, please."

"But your sign says Nelly Longhair costs ten dollars!" Isabel cried out in surprise.

"There's a sales tax," the lady said.

Isabel couldn't believe it. After all that work, she still needed fifty more cents to buy Nelly Longhair! Then she remembered the fifty cents she had started with. She searched around in the bottom of her purse and found it.

Isabel paid the lady exactly ten dollars and
fifty cents, and happily carried Nelly home.

"Sharing" in a Business

Isabel needed money to start a business. So she went to her friends for help. She convinced them to give up their dollars and delay buying things they wanted. She said that if they gave up their dollars to help her start her business, they might make more money later.

Big businesses do something like that when they need money. They will ask people—called "investors"— to give them money to help them with their businesses for the chance of making more money later if their businesses succeed. Sometimes they do this by dividing up their businesses into little pieces and selling some of those pieces to raise money. Those pieces are called "shares of stock."

Let's use Isabel's car wash to show how this works. Imagine that Isabel divides her business into ten pieces. She sells five of those pieces to her friends for one dollar each and keeps five for herself. Her friends now own half of the business, and she owns half. Because her friends own half of the business, she shares half of the $20 she makes by paying them $2 each. This $2 is called a "dividend."

What if Isabel wanted to keep her car wash going? She could pay her friends one dollar instead of two and keep the rest to buy more shammies and soap. Let's say she runs her car wash like this all summer and keeps paying her friends dividends so that they make several dollars more. As Isabel's business makes more money, it becomes more valuable and so do the kids' shares. Seeing how much money Isabel's friends are making, other kids in the neighborhood might want to buy those shares from them. They would probably be willing to pay a lot more than the $1 Isabel's friends paid.

A big business can divide itself up into millions of shares and sell them off for billions of dollars. After it divides itself up and sells the shares, people keep buying and selling the shares among themselves. If a business is successful and makes lots of money, people will want to buy its shares and the price of the shares will go up. If the business is not successful, not many people will want to buy the shares, so the price will go down.

There are places called "stock markets" where people can buy and sell shares of stock. You might have heard of the New York Stock Exchange. I used to work there, and it is one of the biggest stock markets in the world. You can make money in the stock market by buying shares of stock at one price and selling them later for a higher price. You can also lose money if the price of the shares of stock you buy goes down instead of up. The chance that you might lose money is called "risk." Isabel warned her friends that they might lose their dollars if her car wash was not successful. They decided to take the risk of losing the money because her idea was good and because they knew she would work hard.

Isabel's car wash made money right away. But usually it takes years for a big business to start making lots of money. A good example is Amazon.com. (I like that company because I own its stock and because it sells my books.) When Amazon.com got started, it had trouble making money. The price of a share of Amazon.com stock was very low: $2 in 1997. But as I am writing this in October 2007, the company is making lots of money and the price of a share is about $92. If you bought one share of Amazon.com stock in 1997 and sold it in 2007, you would have made $90.

But stocks can go down, too. For a long time, General Motors was a successful business that made many different kinds of automobiles. In the year 2000, the price of a share of stock in General Motors, or "GM," was $71. But since then, GM has had a lot of problems. In October 2007, the price of a share was down to $41. So if you bought a GM share in 2000 and sold it in 2007, you would have lost $30.

When the prices of lots of shares of stock go up, people call it a "bull" market. When the prices of lots of shares of stock go down, they call it a "bear" market. No one is really sure where those words came from, but they have been used for over two hundred years. Some history experts think the words came from the way these animals behave. When a bull catches you, it tosses you up with its horns. When a bear catches you, it pulls you down with its paws!

The prices of stock are published in newspapers every day. Pick a company you like and know about, pretend that you buy a share, and keep track of the price to see whether you are making or losing money.

Remember the most important rules in the stock market:
Buy low.
Sell high.
And don't let those bears get you!